FOG

by **Susi Gregg Fowler**

illustrated by **Jim Fowler**

 Greenwillow Books, New York

TO MY PARENTS, DOUG AND
LILY GREGG, FOR THEIR GIFT
OF MUSIC AND LOVE
     —S. G. F.

TO ANGELA AND MICAELA,
MY FAVORITE MUSIC MAKERS
     —J. F.

Acrylic paints were used for the full-color art.
The text type is Raleigh Medium.

Text copyright © 1992 by Susi Gregg Fowler
Illustrations copyright © 1992 by Jim Fowler
All rights reserved. No part of this book
may be reproduced or utilized in any form
or by any means, electronic or mechanical,
including photocopying, recording, or by
any information storage and retrieval
system, without permission in writing
from the Publisher, Greenwillow Books,
a division of William Morrow & Company, Inc.,
1350 Avenue of the Americas, New York, NY 10019.

Printed in Singapore by Tien Wah Press
First Edition   10 9 8 7 6 5 4 3 2 1

Library of Congress Cataloging-in-Publication Data
Fowler, Susi Gregg.
Fog / by Susi Gregg Fowler ; pictures by Jim Fowler.
p.   cm.
Summary: A visitation by deep fog traps a family in their house
and causes them to rediscover their love of making music.
ISBN 0-688-10593-9 (trade).   ISBN 0-688-10594-7 (lib.)
[1. Fog—Fiction.   2. Family life—Fiction.   3. Music—Fiction.]
I. Fowler, Jim, ill.   II. Title.   PZ7.F8297Fo   1992
[E]—dc20   91-28509   CIP   AC

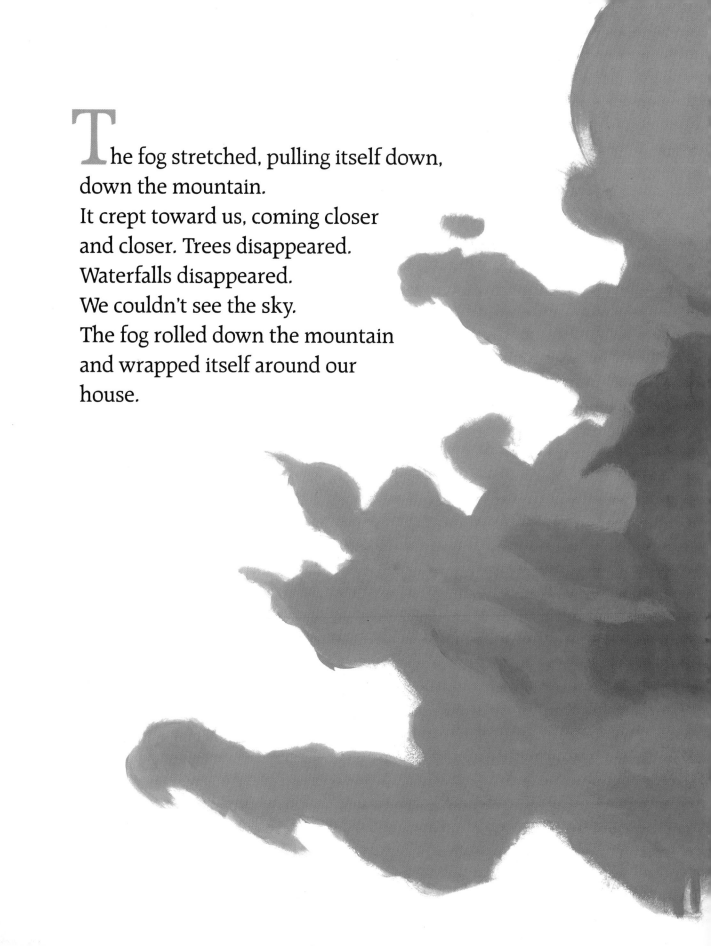

The fog stretched, pulling itself down,
down the mountain.
It crept toward us, coming closer
and closer. Trees disappeared.
Waterfalls disappeared.
We couldn't see the sky.
The fog rolled down the mountain
and wrapped itself around our
house.

I opened the door and stepped outside. It looked like a cloud of silver cotton candy, but it felt cold and wet, not sticky.

My dad said, "This is the worst fog I've ever seen. Better stay inside."

My little sister looked scared. "What's going to happen?" she cried.

"Nothing's going to happen," Momma said, but I could tell she was worried.

"It wants something," said Grandma, pointing
  toward the window.
"It?" I asked.
"The fog," said Grandma.
  Momma shuddered. "I don't like the sound
  of that," she said.
  Happy, our dog, whimpered.
"Hush," said Grandma. We all looked at her.
"We must listen to the fog," she said.

My mother raised her eyebrows, but she didn't say
anything. Daddy shrugged. "What have we got to lose?"
So we all sat around the living room, closed our
eyes, and listened.
It was so quiet, I got the shivers. Then came a sound.

Drip. Drip. Drip.

"The kitchen faucet is still dripping,"
said Daddy. "Maybe the fog wants
it fixed."
"Don't be silly," said Grandma.
"It's not a bad idea, though," said
Momma.
"Shhh," said Grandma with her
finger to her lips.
We were quiet again.

RUSTLE, RUSTLE, RUSTLE.

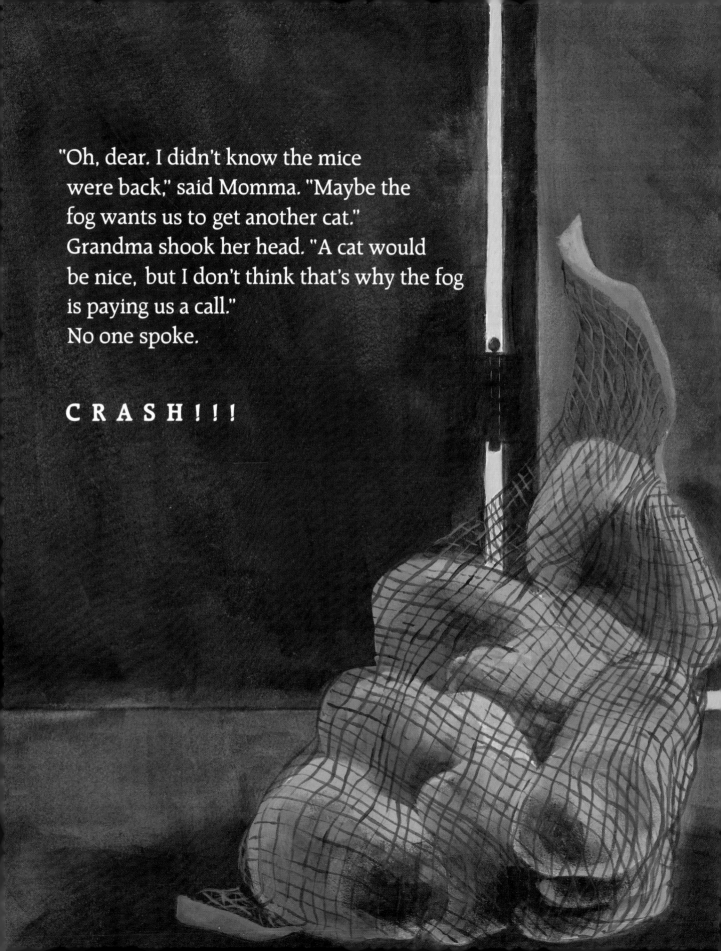

"Oh, dear. I didn't know the mice
were back," said Momma. "Maybe the
fog wants us to get another cat."
Grandma shook her head. "A cat would
be nice, but I don't think that's why the fog
is paying us a call."
No one spoke.

CRASH!!!

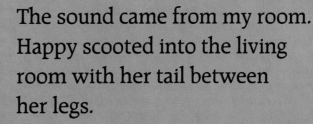

The sound came from my room.
Happy scooted into the living
room with her tail between
her legs.
"I forgot to pick up the block city,"
I explained. "Do you suppose the
fog wants me to clean my room?"
Grandma smiled and shook her
head. "No, but I think Happy does."
Happy settled down by Grandma's
feet and glared at me.
We waited.

Scratch, scratch, scratch.

"Is that the fog?" asked my sister.
"Not the fog—the dog," said Daddy.
"I suppose she's got fleas and needs a bath. Do
 you think that's what the fog is telling us?"
 Happy stood up. "Bath" is one word she knows.
"Well, being quiet is sure showing us what a lot
 of work there is to do." Momma sighed.
"Hush," said Grandma. "I think I'm getting it."

We all looked at Grandma. She squeezed her eyes shut, hunched her shoulders, and leaned toward the window. Every part of her seemed to be listening. Suddenly her eyelids flew open, and she bounced up out of her chair.

"I've got it!" she cried. "Music!"
"Music?" we all said at the same time.
Grandma nodded her head up and down as she
strode across the room. "The fog came for music!"
She picked her fiddle up off the piano. "Come on,
come on," she said.
She was tuning up already.

Momma sat down at the piano and dusted off
the keys. She sneezed. "It's been too long," she
said, laughing.
Daddy picked up his guitar.
I finally found the tambourine under the couch,
and my sister ran into the kitchen for the soup
pot and a wooden spoon.

Soon we were all singing and playing
and laughing and dancing.
Happy was running around in circles—
dog dancing, I guess.

The house didn't seem gloomy and
frightening anymore.
"Look!" I shouted. "Look out the
window!"
It was getting lighter, and now the fog
wasn't creepy.
It began to swirl and curl, to billow
and roll.
"It's dancing! The fog is dancing!"
I cried.

We played all our favorite songs. We played and sang until we were out of tunes and everybody needed something cold to drink. The fog curled and billowed and rolled its way back up the mountain.

"Wow!" said Daddy. "I haven't had so much fun in ages." Momma agreed. "Why don't we play more often? I feel terrific."

Grandma smiled. "I guess we needed reminding."

My little sister ran to the door and called, "Fog—fog! Thank you for coming!"